HENNY-PENNY AND THE SKY IS FALLING

(An English Fairytale)

Retold by Jacquie Hawkins
Illustrated by Dealyne Hawkins

Henny-Penny <u>should</u> have been
<u>Called</u> Miss Scaredy-<u>cat</u>.
<u>She</u> was scared of <u>everything</u>.
That <u>surely</u> was a <u>fact</u>.
She <u>never</u> ever <u>thought</u> things through
So <u>she</u> stayed in <u>confusion.</u>
<u>And</u> she tended <u>always</u> to jump
<u>To</u> some strange <u>conclusions</u>.

One day while she pecked at some small
Crumbs from stale cornbread…….
Something she did not expect to fall
Fell on her head.

Instead of thinking, "I am standing
Underneath a tree,
Therefore it's an acorn that is
Falling down on me"……

She <u>jumped</u> to a <u>conclusion</u> and said,
"<u>Oh</u>, no! Me, O <u>my</u>!
The <u>blue</u> sky must be <u>falling</u> and
So <u>I</u> will surely <u>die</u>!
Why <u>this</u> is a catastrophe! A <u>very</u> dreadful <u>thing</u>!
<u>I</u> must hurry <u>quickly</u> and <u>inform</u> the mighty <u>king</u>!"

So <u>in</u> a hurry <u>off</u> she went,
'But she <u>did</u> not use her <u>brain</u>.
<u>Finally</u> to the <u>house</u> of Cocky <u>Locky</u> <u>Henny came</u>.

Cocky Locky <u>was</u> quite cocky.
That's <u>how</u> he got his <u>name</u>.
<u>He</u> told Henny-<u>Penny</u>," Why <u>you</u> must be <u>insane</u>!
How <u>could</u> the sky be <u>falling</u>, Henny-<u>Penny</u>,
Just on <u>you</u>?
If <u>it</u> was really <u>falling</u>, it'd be <u>falling</u> on me <u>too</u>!"

But, <u>Henny</u> wouldn't <u>listen</u> to his <u>reason</u>
One small <u>bit!</u>
'As <u>she</u> was even <u>more</u> scared than <u>before</u>
She quickly <u>split</u>.

"<u>Cocky</u> Locky's <u>just</u> too <u>cocky</u>,"
<u>She</u> said with a <u>sigh</u>.
"<u>He</u> had better <u>watch</u> out or
He'll <u>be</u> hit with the <u>sky</u>!
And <u>just</u> because the <u>sky</u> has never
<u>Fallen</u> on him <u>yet</u>
<u>Doesn't</u> mean that <u>it</u> won't fall on <u>him</u> soon,
I <u>regret</u>."

<u>She</u> found Ducky <u>Daddles</u> swimming
<u>Slowly</u> on a <u>pond</u>.....

She yelled out her story…but he did not respond.
He was just too busy to care much anyway.
That the sky would ever fall from
Up there to the ground
Was so absurd that Ducky Duddles…
Wouldn't have believed it anyway.

So Henny-Penny shook her head
And left without a sound,
Leaving Ducky Duddles there
Swimming on the pond.
She mumbled…."Ducky Duddles
Is so busy he can't see
That the sky is truly falling and he
Certainly should flee!"

She gave it no further thought
And quickly sped away
Until she noticed Goosey Lucy
Who headed her way.

She was busy chasing
A handsome, pure white gander
And had no time for Henny-Penny....
Or any bystander.

But, <u>Henny</u>-Penny <u>cried</u> out to her,
"<u>You</u> had better <u>run</u>
For the <u>sky</u> is surely <u>falling</u> and it <u>will</u> kill <u>everyone!</u>
<u>Goosey</u> Lucy only <u>stopped</u>
<u>Long</u> enough for <u>a</u> few <u>words</u>.
"Why <u>Henny</u>-Penny <u>that's</u> the silliest <u>thing</u>
I ever <u>heard!</u>"

Goosey honked once in disgust
And then took up the chase,
Leaving Henny fuming...and staring into space.
Henny-Penny mumbled,
"There is nothing I can do.
I guess she is entitled
To have her silly view."

So <u>Henny</u> went on <u>down</u> the road
Till <u>she</u> heard, "Gobble, <u>gobble</u>."
<u>There</u> sat Turkey <u>Lurkey</u>
In the <u>middle</u> of a <u>squabble</u>.
<u>Her</u> four little <u>gobblers</u> were <u>busy</u> fussing <u>madly</u>
And <u>Henny</u>-Penny <u>sure</u> agreed....
That <u>they</u> behaved quite <u>badly</u>.

But <u>Henny</u>-Penny <u>was</u> so <u>scared</u>
<u>That</u> the sky would <u>fall</u>
<u>That</u> she didn't <u>give</u> much thought
To the <u>gobbler</u> squabble…<u>not</u> at all.
<u>But</u> she told the <u>little</u> poults,
"<u>You</u> had best be<u>have</u>
For the <u>sky</u> will soon be <u>falling</u>
If the <u>King</u> the world can't <u>save</u>!"

The <u>last</u> thing she <u>remembered</u> was
The <u>gobblers</u> looking <u>up.</u>

<u>As</u> she quickly <u>sped</u> away she <u>said</u>, "With any <u>luck</u>

<u>I</u> will get to <u>tell</u> the king (<u>If</u> I am in <u>time</u>)
<u>So</u> he'll stop the <u>sky</u> from falling.
I'll <u>be</u> back home by <u>bedtime</u>.

But then Foxy <u>Loxy</u> stopped her
<u>On</u> the way to <u>say</u>,
"<u>What</u> is your big <u>hurry</u>?
Why not <u>for</u> a minute <u>stay</u>?"
So <u>Henny</u>-Penny <u>told</u> the fox,
"<u>I</u> must save the <u>world</u>,
And <u>stop</u> the sky from <u>falling</u>
Be<u>fore</u> to earth it's <u>hurled</u>!"

Unlike Henny <u>that</u> sly fox <u>surely</u> used his <u>brain</u>.
He <u>knew</u> the sky would <u>never</u> fall
To <u>earth</u> just like the <u>rain</u>
<u>But</u> he did not <u>tell</u> her <u>exactly</u> all he <u>knew</u>
For <u>he</u> thought tender <u>chicken</u>
Would <u>make</u> a yummy <u>stew</u>.

Foxy acted <u>like</u> he trusted <u>each</u> word that she <u>said</u>
And <u>believed</u> the <u>sky</u> would <u>soon</u> be falling
<u>On</u> top of their <u>heads</u>.
<u>He</u> told Henny, "<u>I</u> know of a <u>short</u>-cut that will <u>bring</u>
Us <u>where</u> we want to <u>go</u>..
Right to the <u>doorstep</u> of the <u>king</u>."

He <u>led</u> her to his <u>house</u>…
And <u>then</u> into his <u>den</u>
<u>Telling</u> her, "The <u>king's</u> door's in
The <u>hallway</u> at the <u>end</u>."
As <u>Foxy</u> led that <u>silly</u> hen down
<u>Through</u> the hall he <u>knew</u>
<u>That</u> before too <u>very</u> long
He'd <u>have</u> his chicken <u>stew</u>.

The <u>moral</u> of the <u>story</u> is
That <u>you</u> must use your <u>head</u>
And <u>not</u> go off <u>half</u> cocked.
You'd better <u>think</u> things through in<u>stead</u>.

And <u>if</u> your friends all <u>dis</u>agree
<u>With</u> you right <u>along</u>….
It <u>just</u> may be that <u>they</u> are right…
And <u>you're</u> the one that's <u>wrong</u>.

OTHER FAIRYTALES WITH A BEAT:

THE LITTLE RED HEN
THE TRAVELING FOX
GOLDILOCKS

LOOK FOR OTHER FAIRYTALES WITH A BEAT
TO COME OUT SOON.

Made in United States
Orlando, FL
18 August 2023

36234664R00018